THE TREE OF TIME

A Story of a Special Sequoia

by Kathy Baron

YOSEMITE
ASSOCIATION

YOSEMITE NATIONAL PARK, CALIFORNIA

Yosemite Association
P.O. Box 545
Yosemite National Park, CA 95389

PRINTED IN HONG KONG

ISBN 0-939666-73-1

Design by Robin Weiss.

Dedicated to Mom, and in loving
memory of Walter Ciejka, my Dad.
Thank you for taking me camping
in the Sierras every summer.

Once upon a time, in a cool, silent forest, a bright-eyed chickaree jostled a round, brown sequoia cone, causing a tiny seed to fall out.

The tiny seed had stiff little wings, and it sailed along with the breeze until it landed gently on a spot of bare soil.

Soon snow covered the seed, pressing it to the ground. Before long, even underneath the snow, the shell of the seed split open, and a tiny root thrust itself against the frozen earth.

By the time the snow had melted, a little sprout was already reaching up toward the warm spring sunshine.

At about the same time that the little sprout's life was beginning, far away on the other side of the world, a brilliant general named Hannibal was carrying out a plan for a bold surprise attack. He marched 26,000 men and 37 war elephants over the Alps into Italy, trying in vain to defeat the powerful Roman army.

300–280 B.C.	270 B.C.	250 B.C.	218 B.C.
The Colossus of Rhodes, a huge statue of the sun god, was built by the Greeks.	Greek astronomer Aristarchus stated that the Earth revolves around the Sun.	Archimedes, a Greek mathematician, outlined the laws of specific gravity.	Hannibal crossed the Alps.

He didn't know about the
new little sprout emerging
from the snow so far away.

Meanwhile, the little sprout began to grow — about two inches its first year. It turned a deep healthy green and sent strong roots down into the rich earth.

Seasons passed, and the tiny plant grew into a cone-shaped young sapling, with prickly needles and a rough brown bark. By its fifteenth birthday, the tree was growing its own cones and seeds.

東日來門丰

Far away across the sea, the Han Dynasty ruled in splendor over the people of China. Art, education, and science flourished. Paper was invented. Ideas and merchandise were traded freely with Roman citizens. The borders of the vast Chinese nation were securely protected by a newly-finished Great Wall over 1,500 miles long.

The Han emperors knew nothing of the graceful young tree in the distant land across the ocean.

246 B.C.–250 A.D.	215 B.C.	202 B.C.–9 A.D.	200 B.C.	140 B.C.	133–122 B.C.
The Roman Empire was at its height.	The Great Wall of China was built.	The Han Dynasty was at its height.	Mayan tribes began to settle the jungles of Central America.	The statue called the Venus de Milo was created by an unknown Greek artist.	Civil war was waged in Rome.

The little tree grew taller
and taller—to over 150
feet—as the years passed by.

Hail Caesar! The roar from the crowd in a faraway land was deafening. A strong man dressed in white robes stepped forward to receive the adulation. He was Julius Caesar, ruler of the Roman Empire. Huge armies marched, battles were fought, magnificent buildings were erected, and beautiful artworks were created in his honor.

Even Caesar didn't know about the tall young tree.

100 B.C.   65 B.C.   51–30 B.C.   45 B.C.

Basket-making   In Rome, Julius Caesar   Cleopatra ruled as   Julius Caesar
people lived in   introduced public games,   Queen of Egypt.   became the sole
America's south-   including chariot races,   ruler of the
west region.   and became very popular.   Roman Empire.

In the hush of the deep
forest, the tree continued
to grow. It was so large
now that its own top
branches shadowed its
base. The lack of light
had long since caused the
lower branches to die
and fall off, and the tree's
trunk was straight and tall.

Thousands and
thousands of miles away,
a baby named Jesus was
born in a manger outside
the town of Bethlehem.

4 B.C.–30 A.D.	43 A.D.	60 A.D.	79 A.D.	90 A.D.	105 A.D.
Jesus Christ lived and spread his teachings.	The Romans invaded Britain.	Buddhism reached China from Asia and India.	Pompeii was destroyed by a volcano.	The Great Silk Road (2,500 miles long) was traveled by merchants across Asia to Persia.	The Chinese made the first paper from vegetable fibers.

The maturing tree grew
bigger. Its rough, brown
bark had deepened to a
rich red color.

The years passed, and, a world away, the followers of Jesus were persecuted. The mighty Roman Empire began its fall.

117–138

200–300

286

300–500

300–600

Hadrian traveled around the British Empire and built Hadrian's Wall.

The first wheelbarrows were used in China.

The Roman Empire was divided.

Great mounds were built by the Hopewell Indians in North America.

The Mayans experienced their Golden Age.

The tree continued growing. It was nearly 200 feet tall, and its shallow roots spread out 100 feet in every direction. Indians gathered food and hunted under its shady boughs.

Across the sea, a wise man named Mohammed taught his people about their Creator. Nomads gathered in the vast desert to hear his inspiring words. The nations of Europe entered the Dark Ages. Monks kept alive the wisdom of western civilization, laboriously copying books by hand, while peasants struggled to survive a harsh daily existence.

370–476   400   432–590   451   570–631   618–755

The Fall of Rome resulted from attacks by barbarians.

Early Christian missionaries were sent out to convert non-believers.

A rich feudal society developed in Japan.

Attila the Hun and followers attacked France and northern Italy.

Mohammed lived and taught.

The Tang Dynasty was at its height in China.

And the tree grew bigger. Each year it produced over 1,500 cones, and with the help of chickarees, released hundreds of thousands of tiny seeds.

During the distant celebration of a cold, clear Christmas Day, Charlemagne was crowned King of the Holy Roman Empire. His nation was strong and secure. Castles were built. Generations of serfs toiled for their feudal lords, while knights jousted and fought.

700–875

742–814

750

800

850

Vikings from Norway and Denmark crossed the ocean to Iceland and Greenland.

Charlemagne lived and ruled the Holy Roman Empire.

The first clock was invented in China.

Feudal society was common and important in Europe.

The first Russian states were founded.

The tree grew taller still, and its trunk was massive and wide. Its spongy, red bark was over a foot thick, protecting it from the forest fires and insect attacks that killed many of the neighboring trees.

On the other side of the world, medieval craftsmen fitted in the last stones to complete the Cathedral of Notre Dame. Christian Crusaders marched again and again to battle the followers of Mohammed, in the hopes of gaining control over the land where Jesus had lived.

900

990

1000

1096–1270

1100–1400

1163

1174

The Mayans moved to the Yucatan Peninsula.

The Samurai class was at the center of Japanese life.

North America's first city, Cahokia, was built near St. Louis.

Thousands of castles were built throughout Europe.

The Cathedral of Notre Dame was completed.

The Italians began to build the Tower of Pisa.

The Christian Crusades were carried out.

The tree lived on,
growing more majestic
with every passing
season. As it aged, some
of the limbs in its crown
died and broke off.

The Renaissance began in Europe, and western civilization reached a new pinnacle of learning and culture. Michelangelo sculpted the statue of David, and Leonardo da Vinci painted the Mona Lisa. The European people began to explore their planet, and soon Columbus "discovered" America.

1206–1227

1254–1324

1300

1347

1431

1490s

1492

Marco Polo traveled the world and explored China.

The Aztecs settled in central Mexico and became very powerful.

Black Death, a form of the plague, killed one-third of the people in Europe.

Joan of Arc was burnt as a witch in France.

Christopher Columbus landed in America.

Genghis Khan conquered much of China, Persia, Poland, India and Russia.

Leonardo da Vinci painted the Mona Lisa.

The tree spread its
enormous branches
over the quiet forest.

Spanish conquistadors and English pioneers crossed the ocean, coming for the first time to the vast land where the big tree stood. In search of gold, power, and freedom, they settled over the American continents, killing the native people who stood in their way.

BARON

1519–1600   1556–1605   1564–1616   1579   1600–1699   1620   1650–1750   1689

Spanish conquista-
dors settled North
and South America,
establishing
colonies there.

William Shakespeare
lived and wrote his
many plays and poems.

Akbar the Great ruled India.

Ottoman Turks occupied
Central Europe, the Middle
East and North Africa.

Sir Francis Drake, sailor and
adventurer, claimed California
for the English.

Philosophers like Voltaire
and Rousseau spawned The
Enlightenment.

The Mayflower   Peter the Great
landed at   seized total
Plymouth Rock,   power in Russia.
Massachusetts.

The tree was still growing, but more slowly now. It had reached the height of a 23-story building and weighed as much as 14 train locomotives. It lived on, one of over 200 individual trees in a grove of sequoia giants.

"We the people of the United States, in order to form a more perfect Union…" The air fairly crackled with excitement as 55 great men gathered in Independence Hall to establish the form of government for their new nation.

1750–1850

1787

The U.S. Constitution was written.

The developement of new machines led to the Industrial Revolution in Britain.

1789–1799

High taxes and poor living conditions resulted in the French Revolution.

1804–1821

Napoleon was the Emperor of France and controlled most of Western Europe.

1812–1859

Australia was settled.

1848

The Gold Rush brought thousands of fortune hunters to California.

European pioneers found the big tree grove, and soon its silence was shattered by the thundering boom of logging operations in distant mountains.

Two thousand miles away, brother fought brother in a bloody Civil War. Abraham Lincoln signed the Emancipation Proclamation, ending the practice of slavery in the United States.

1859

Charles Darwin published "The Origin of Species."

1859–1868

The Suez Canal was built in Egypt.

1861–1865

The Civil War was fought in the United States.

1863

The Emancipation Proclamation, freeing all slaves, was issued by Abraham Lincoln.

1864

The Mariposa Grove and Yosemite Valley were protected as a state reserve.

1866

Swedish chemist, Alfred Nobel, invented dynamite.

1866–1900

The German Empire was on the rise.

The logging operations grew closer and closer to the tree. Some people cried out that the tree, as well as the others in the grove, must be protected. They named this group of sequoias the Mariposa Grove and asked that the area be set aside as a state reserve. The U.S. Congress agreed, and the grove was spared.

The tree was still growing. People were impressed with what they had heard about the size of the ancient giants, and wanted to see the trees for themselves. The big tree was selected from among all the sequoias in the Mariposa Grove to be a special attraction.

1867
The United States bought Alaska from Russia.

1868
The skull of Cro-Magnon man was unearthed by Louis Lartet.

1873
Remington mass-produced the first typewriter.

1876
Alexander Bell invented the first telephone.

A 26-foot-long tunnel was cut through the heart of the tree to allow stagecoaches to pass through its mammoth trunk. It was named the "Wawona Tree," using an Indian word describing the hooting of the owls that lived among the giant sequoias.

The whole Mariposa Grove, including the Wawona Tree, was added to the newly-created Yosemite National Park.

1881	1889	1890	1896	1906	1908	1914–1918	1920	1937

The tunnel was cut in the Wawona "Tunnel" Tree.

The Eiffel tower was built in Paris.

The first modern Olympic Games were held in Athens, Greece.

Yosemite National Park was established

World War I disrupted Western Europe.

Henry Ford made the first Model "T" car.

The Mariposa Grove and Yosemite Valley became part of Yosemite National Park.

The German airship, The Hindenburg, was destroyed by fire.

Mohandas Ghandi preached civil disobedience in India.

Although weakened by the tunnel, the tree lived on and became one of Yosemite's most popular sights.

Then one spring day in 1969, just a few months before astronauts landed on the moon, the huge Wawona Tree toppled over into the powdery snow.

The tree had not been the largest sequoia, nor the oldest. But it had thrived in the grove for 2,200 years, while humans had gone from horse-drawn chariots to rockets on the moon.

1939–1945   1945   1954   1955   1957   1963

The United Nations was created.

Roger Bannister ran the first sub-four-minute mile.

Rock 'n roll music was born.

The first satellite, Sputnik I, orbited the Earth.

President John F. Kennedy was assassinated.

The Second World War ended with the dropping of atomic bombs on Japan.

No one was there to
see the tree fall. Its life
ended as it had begun,
with only the quiet forest
as witness.

1969	1975	1976	1981	1986
Two American astronauts walked on the surface of the moon.	The first personal computer was produced.	A supersonic airplane, the Concorde, began flights across the Atlantic Ocean.	The first space shuttle, Columbia, orbited the Earth.	A nuclear disaster occured at the Chernobyl power plant in the U.S.S.R.

And today the Wawona Tree lies there still, a giant, fallen tree of time in an ancient grove of sequoia trees.